Animal Orphans

Animal Orphans

created by
Sharon M. Hart

written by
Avery Hart and Paul Mantell

illustrated by
Sandy Rabinowitz

A
LITTLE APPLE
PAPERBACK

A Parachute Press Book

SCHOLASTIC INC.

New York   Toronto   London   Auckland   Sydney

ISBN 0-590-41502-6

12 11 10 9 8 7 6 5 4 3 2   9/8 0 1 2 3/9

Printed in the U.S.A.   11
First Scholastic printing, December 1988

Contents

Something Important / 1

Emergency! / 9

Into the Everglades / 17

The Tiny Twins / 28

The Cubs Come Home / 35

Missing! / 49

Out in the Storm / 61

Back to Nature / 76

Letting Go / 89

Queen of the Wild / 99

To Clayton and Matthew Mantell

Chapter One

———•———

Something Important

Dear Mom and Dad — I hate it here.

No, that was all wrong. That wasn't what he meant to say at all. Eleven-year-old Timothy Quinn put his pen down and looked out the window. The red sun was just going down over River Oaks, the animal rescue farm his grandparents had created to help animals in need.

The big Florida sky had lavender and pink streaks all over it. From cypress branches, clumps of Spanish moss blew like gray beards in the breeze.

Tim heard a lion roaring in the distance. It had to be Raj. Rudy the gamekeeper had just headed out to feed the big cats and change their straw for the night. *If only I could go with him and help*, Tim thought.

Over in the far meadow, Tim could see his nine-year-old sister Arden riding her horse Glory. He couldn't see the smile on Arden's face, but he guessed it was there. Arden and Glory had been a team ever since Gramp brought the black filly to River Oaks.

With a sigh, Tim turned back to his letter. Crumpling the paper into a ball, he tossed it onto the floor, took a fresh sheet, and tried again.

Dear Mom and Dad — I don't hate it here, but I don't have anything to do anymore. . . .

A burst of laughter from downstairs interrupted Tim's thought. Jesse was showing off one of Mortie the mynah bird's new tricks to Gran and Gramp. Tim liked Mortie, too, but lately the salty old bird was the only thing his little brother seemed to care about.

Tim knew that Arden and Jesse loved it here at River Oaks. But his brother and sister had no idea how unhappy *he* was, and Tim didn't want them to find out. After all, he was the oldest, and he was supposed to be the leader.

Tim folded his arms on the desk and buried his chin in them. Connecticut seemed a million miles away, and a whole year away from home seemed like forever. All his friends had probably forgotten him already. He hadn't gotten a letter from anybody in days.

As for his parents, they were off touring Africa, taking photographs and writing articles about endangered wildlife for their magazine. Tim was proud of them, but he still felt lonely.

At home, if he felt bad, he could always talk to Mom and Dad. But here at River Oaks, what could he do? Gran and Gramp were great, but it just wasn't the same.

When Tim lifted his head again, the first stars of night were beaming.

There was the North Star, hanging right over the recovery barn. Tim wondered if his mother and father were seeing the very same star from their camp in Africa, and whether they were thinking of him.

Dear Mom and Dad —

"Tim! Hi!" Arden was standing at the door. "How come you didn't come to the stable after supper?"

"I wanted to write a letter."

Immediately Arden's brown eyes zoomed to the paper on the desk. Just as quickly, Tim covered it with his arm.

But he had forgotten about the rejected sheets on the floor. Arden swooped down and picked one up.

"Hey, that's private!" said Tim, too late.

" 'I hate it here'. . .?" Arden couldn't

believe what she read. "Tim, what's going on? I thought you liked it here."

"I do," Tim lied. "It's just. . . ."

"Just what?" Arden asked.

"Well, I thought I was coming here to learn how to be an 'animals man,' " Tim finally said. "That's what Gramp called it. Everything was fine when I had the chimps to work with, but they got sent away!"

"What about the anhingas? I thought you were feeding them," said Arden.

"You mean the chickens of the Everglades?" Tim muttered. "I didn't come here to play with chickens, Arden."

"Hmph," Arden sniffed, tossing her long brown ponytail. "Chickens are as important as any other animals, and you know it."

"Not to me," Tim insisted.

"Then what? Which animals *would* you want to work with?"

Tim looked up at the drawings he'd made of Raj and the other big cats in their habitat. Arden saw his glance, and her brown eyes opened wide.

"The cats are much too dangerous," she protested. "You know that!"

Tim threw down his pen with a sigh. "Too dangerous, too dangerous. Everybody agrees. But how am I supposed to learn anything around here if Gran and Gramp won't even give me a chance?" he demanded. "I'm not a kid anymore, but they keep treating me like one!"

Arden looked her brother up and down. It wasn't like him to complain. "Tim, what's wrong with being a kid?" she asked softly.

Tim was so annoyed, he could barely answer. "Aw, what do you know about it? You're only nine! And besides, you've had Glory to take care of, right from the start."

He sighed and picked up his pen. "I'm going to ask Mom and Dad to let me meet them in Africa," he said. "I don't want to be stuck here for a whole year."

"They won't say yes," said Arden.

"So maybe you should make the best of it here. We're really lucky to be at River Oaks, and you know it!"

Tim gritted his teeth. Arden was usually a great sister, but this time she just didn't understand.

"Besides," she coaxed, "we're going on our picnic tomorrow — that'll be fun."

"Who cares about a stupid picnic?" said Tim, not really meaning it. The picnic at the Indian Mounds was something he'd been looking forward to for ages.

"Tim, why are you being so mean?" asked Arden, looking hurt.

"Oh, forget it!" he said finally, turning his head to avoid his sister's gaze. "Just leave me alone, okay?"

Arden blinked back tears and tilted her face to one side. "I'll leave," she murmured, her lip trembling. "But I think you're being silly. And they're still not going to let you go to Africa," she repeated, closing the door behind her.

When she was gone, Tim tried to

write his parents again, but he couldn't. Every time he put pen to paper, Arden's words came back to him: *We're really lucky to be here.* . . .

Crumpling up one more sheet, he threw it on the floor with all the others. Nobody understood him. Not Arden, not Gramp, not Gran, not Jesse, not even his parents.

All he wanted was to do something *important*. What was so wrong with *that*?

Chapter Two

———•———

Emergency!

"Come on, Gran! Come on, everybody! We'll be late!" Jesse's excited voice shot through the kitchen.

Tansy Quinn smiled. "Don't worry, Jesse, the Indian Mounds will still be there, even if we're a little late."

The Indian Mounds were a very special place. Before the settlers came to Florida, the Indians were said to have buried their dead there. Some people thought the Mounds were haunted, but Gramp said that was nonsense. If people treated the place with respect, there was no reason to be frightened. Still, it was a little spooky to be going there.

"Getting a group like this to a picnic is no easy matter," said Gran as she packed sandwiches into the wicker picnic basket. "Arden, would you get some napkins from the pantry?"

"Sure, Gran," said Arden.

"Well, that's about it," Gramp said, turning the lid on the big red Thermos. "Where's Tim?"

"He's outside already," Jesse replied, his eyes on the cookies Gran was packing now. "How come he was so weird this morning?"

"I don't know," Gran said. "But I guess when Tim wants to tell us what's bothering him, he will."

Tim hadn't said a word to anyone all morning. Jesse and Gran didn't understand it, but Arden did. Tim was still as sad and angry as he'd been the night before.

"You know, I really should stay home and fix that porch screen," Gramp said as they walked out into the sunshine. "Otherwise, we'll have a house full of mosquitoes tonight!"

"Forget it, Gramp," laughed Arden. "Today is a day of *no work* — you promised. You can fix it Monday. Besides, Tim and I put cardboard over the hole yesterday afternoon."

"Well, that's something anyway," Gramp said. "Now, is everybody ready for a picnic?"

"Yay!" shouted Arden and Jesse, flying to the old tan station wagon. Tim was already sitting in the back, munching on a long blade of grass and staring blankly out the window.

Gramp started the engine, and Jesse scrambled in beside Tim. Just then, the phone rang inside the house.

"I'll get it," said Gran, who was just coming down the path.

"Oh, no! Don't answer, Gran!" Jesse yelled through the car window. Tansy Quinn was a veterinarian, and emergency calls always seemed to come at the wrong time.

"But Jesse, someone may need my

11

help," Gran answered. "It's probably nothing," she said, disappearing into the house.

Arden slid into the seat on the other side of Tim. But he was too busy looking at the palmetto plants on the road to notice her. *How long is he going to keep this up?* she wondered, finally turning away. If he wanted to be like that, there was nothing she could do about it.

When Gran came out again, she was carrying her black medical bag and walking very fast. She seemed worried as she got into the car.

"Thomas," she told Gramp, "there's a problem in the Everglades."

Gramp reached down and picked up the microphone of the CB radio. "Huey, get the chopper ready. The Doc has a call. Over."

"Ten-four, and out," came the static-filled response from about a mile and a half away.

"Heliport, here we come," said Gramp, pulling away from the house.

"Kids, I'm sorry about the picnic, but this is really important," Gran said.

"I'll *never* get to the Indian Mounds!" Jesse moaned from the backseat.

"Jesse, a Florida panther's been hurt. That's always an emergency," said Gran.

"Why, Gran?" asked Arden.

"Florida panthers are terribly endangered," Gran explained. "There are only about thirty left. If we're not careful, we could lose the entire species."

"Can that really happen?" Jesse asked.

"Yes, it can, Jesse, and it does. In fact, it happens far too often," said Gramp, turning onto the heliport grounds. "Don't worry, Tansy," he told his wife. "We'll get you there in time."

"There's Huey. Looks like he's all ready to fly. Kids, take good care of your grandfather for me. I'll get back as soon as I can." And then she was out of the car, running to the chopper.

" 'Bye!" everyone called out — everyone but Tim. He ran after his grandmother and caught her by the arm. "Gran!

13

Wait! Let me come with you!"

Tansy Quinn spun around in surprise. "You want to come? Are you sure?" she asked, searching Tim's eager green eyes. "There may be a lot of waiting around and — "

"Please, Gran. Maybe I can help."

"What's going on?" asked Gramp, catching up with them.

"Tim wants to come, Thomas. . . ." Tim's grandparents gave each other a long look before Gran turned back to Tim. "Okay," she said, one foot already on the step of the waiting chopper. "Hop on."

"Hold it!" cried Arden, who'd heard every word. "What about *me*?"

"I suppose I can't say no to you when I just said yes to your brother," Gran said.

"Me, too!" yelled Jesse. "I want to go, too!"

Gran and Gramp shot each other another look — a quick one this time. Jesse didn't have a chance.

14

"Now, wait a minute, Sport," said Gramp with a smile. "I need someone to help me hold down the fort while your grandmother is gone! There are several hundred hungry mouths to feed at River Oaks, you know. *You've* got to help me out — be my special assistant for the day. We have an awful lot to do. Now that the picnic's off, I think we should start by picking up that lost dog Mayor Whitlam called about last night."

"You mean the Irish setter?" asked Jesse, perking up. "The one who's been wandering around downtown with the cut on her leg?"

"Yup, I do. The mayor wants Gran to take a look at it, and I said we'd keep the dog till somebody comes to claim her. Shouldn't take long if she's as beautiful as they say."

"Okay, Gramp," said Jesse. "I'll stay with you."

"Doc, the chopper's ready," said Huey, putting on his earphones.

"Well, come on if you're coming,"

Gran told Tim and Arden. "There's a panther waiting for us out in the wild!"

Tim was already in the helicopter. Now *this* was something else. He was finally doing something important!

Chapter Three

———•———

Into the Everglades

"Elevator . . . going up!" Gran yelled over the noise of the engine. "Take a deep breath, kids. It helps."

The 'copter shot up into the air, and Tim's stomach shot up to the ceiling. He'd been bounced off the ground, and now there was only a bubble of clear plastic between him and the sky.

"Wow!" Tim panted. It was thrilling but scary to be where you felt you could step out into the clouds.

Tansy flashed her grandchildren a smile. "You won't fall out, I promise," she assured them.

"How far away are the Everglades, Gran?" Arden asked.

17

"Under an hour by helicopter, but it would have taken forever by road," Gran replied.

Tim and Arden looked down. Below them, the streets and roads had ended. There were a few foot trails and some light wooden bridges for traveling, but not many. The world of civilization had suddenly stopped — and the Everglades had begun.

"Get a good look, because there's no place on earth like it," Gran shouted over the engine's roar. "The Indians called it the River of Grass, and you can see why."

Arden and Tim were looking down at a plain of thick, green saw grass dotted with dark clumps of cypress and gumbo-limbo trees. Shadows of clouds moved over the vegetation in everchanging patterns. Under and through the reeds, they caught glimpses of water sparkling in the sun.

"The water here doesn't run very deep," Gran said. "Most of what you see is no more than six inches, but it flows

across the entire peninsula of Florida. The Glades rest on a bed of limestone that's as flat as a table. It slopes ever so gently, and takes water all the way to the Gulf of Mexico."

"What are those big dark places?" asked Tim, pressing his face against the bubble of the chopper.

"Those are clumps of hardwood trees, Tim. We call them tree islands, and they actually hold the earth together. They're mostly cypress and gumbo-limbo, but you can find trees from all over the world here, too. The seeds blow in on the wind, and birds carry them here from as far away as Vermont and South America! There's an incredible mixture of plant life."

Tim and Arden spent the rest of the journey staring at the lush landscape below them. They barely noticed when the chopper began drifting down toward the landing pad beside the ranger station.

"Good luck, Doc," said Huey after he'd brought the big machine to a halt and shut down the engine. "You kids are lucky. Not many people ever get to see a genuine Florida panther."

As they stepped onto the tarmac, a young ranger came running up to them. "Dr. Quinn, are we ever glad to see you," he said.

"Hi, Pete. Meet my grandchildren, Arden and Tim. They're here to help, too," Gran said as they hurriedly followed the ranger to his waiting airboat.

"It's a female," the ranger told Gran. "She was hit by a camper on Loop Road, over by Pinecrest. I can have you there in ten minutes."

Tim climbed into the flat motorized boat they'd be using. It had a big propeller at the back and was perfect for traveling over shallow waters.

As the boat cast off, whooshing along the thick fringe of shoreline plants, Tim took a deep breath of tropical air. At last — he was on a real adventure!

They arrived just minutes later and hiked to the edge of Loop Road, where several park rangers were standing in a tight cluster. When they saw Dr. Quinn approaching, they made way.

Following right behind Gran, Tim and Arden got their first look at the rare Florida panther. She was lying on the side of the road. A huge, tawny creature with eyes of pure gold, she had cinnamon-colored stripes across her face and delicate markings on her muscular body.

Nature had made the panther lean, sleek, and strong. She was smart, too. Smart enough to be at the top of the food chain. Her only real enemy was man, with his guns, his bulldozers — and his automobiles.

Tim could see where the car must have hit the big cat. She had a mean-looking gash that went all the way from her shoulder to her hind leg.

Tim had a feeling the panther knew Gran was there to help her. She looked up at the vet with pleading eyes.

"I'll anesthetize her," Gran said, "and we'll operate right here. This animal's not in any shape to travel."

Tansy Quinn was in charge now. Before Arden could look away, Gran had given the panther a tranquilizer from a long needle. Then Gran handed one of the rangers a small bottle of rubbing alcohol and a package of sterilized gauze. "Would you wipe the portable operating table with this alcohol?" she asked.

The other rangers gently picked up

the panther and laid her on the long, flat table for surgery.

"She's definitely of breeding age," Gran pointed out as she put on her surgical gloves.

"What does that mean, Gran?" asked Arden.

"It means she can have babies, Arden. In fact, if I'm right, this panther has given birth pretty recently," Gran sighed sadly. "And that means we'll lose the whole family."

"Why, Gran?" This time it was Tim who asked.

"Well, Tim, panther babies can't survive without their mothers. It's as simple as that. In the wild, a panther mother will stay with her young for nearly two years. It takes them that long to learn how to hunt. Without a parent to teach them, the cubs become easy prey for alligators and other hungry predators."

"You mean her babies will *die* if she dies?" asked Arden softly.

Gran nodded regretfully. "I'm afraid

24

so, Arden. We could lose up to three or four panthers, just because of one careless human being. We'll probably never even find the cubs. Panther mothers hide their dens extremely well. Even experts have a hard time locating them."

When she was ready to operate, Gran gave Tim and Arden a choice. "You can stay here, but you've got to be completely silent. Or, you can wait over there by the boat. It's up to you."

Arden decided to wait by the boat. The sight of blood made her feel weak and funny inside.

Tim said he'd stay and watch, but when Gran took out her instruments, he had second thoughts. For a minute, all he wanted to do was turn around and shut his eyes. He didn't, though. With his heart pounding, he stood there as if hypnotized.

Suddenly Gran wasn't Gran anymore. She was Dr. Tansy Quinn, expert surgeon of big cats, member of the Panther Recovery Program, who'd trained in Africa and practiced her skills her whole adult life.

Without any show of emotion, Gran pierced the panther with a small, sharp knife and opened up the animal's sleek fur.

Arden prayed silently as she stood by the boat waiting, *Please, please let her be all right.*

But it wasn't to be. Only minutes later Gran took off her surgical mask and shook her head. "She's gone," she announced softly. "There was nothing we could have done to save her. The chest cavity was crushed beyond repair."

Everyone was stunned.

Tim felt a lump grow in his throat as he watched the rangers take the panther away.

"We'll start back for River Oaks right now," Gran murmured to him softly. "There's nothing more we can do here." Her lips pursed, she began packing up her instruments.

26

Tim had never seen Gran look so defeated.

Just then, the Quinns heard voices shouting in the distance. Tim and Gran looked up in time to see two field assistants running toward them. Each was carrying a tiny bundle of fur.

"The cubs!" one of the rangers shouted jubilantly. "We found them! We found the cubs!"

Chapter Four

———•———

The Tiny Twins

"They're so little!" Arden could hardly believe it. The spotted cubs were just the size of small puppies, and their milky blue eyes were barely open. Compared to their six-foot-long mother, the orphans were absolutely tiny.

"We found them about a hundred yards off the road," one of the field assistants was telling Gran. "Pete noticed an alligator acting pretty strange in a cluster of gumbo-limbo trees. He was definitely stalking something. And sure enough — there they were! They weren't at all afraid."

"Tiny cubs like this are too young to know fear," said Gran, reaching out and stroking one of the panthers, "and they're used to having a mother around."

"They look like leopards," said Tim.

"Yes, they do, but they'll lose those spots when they're about six months," Gran explained, scratching the other cub behind the ears.

"Dr. Quinn, do they have any chance at all?" Pete asked. Everyone waited for the answer.

Gran frowned. "Last year we were able to save a couple of seven-month-olds. But we've never seen any cubs this young. I don't think they could be more than two weeks old."

Gran reached out and picked up one of the panthers. "Well, I must say, this one has a strong heartbeat. She seems like a good eater, too. Let's see, any teeth in there? Open up, honey."

Gran pulled gently on the little panther's jaw. The tiny mouth was bright pink and the gums were smooth and soft. "No teeth yet, not even knobs. I suppose it's possible that she *might* be able to make it as a domestic animal. It's worth a try, anyway. They're very affectionate creatures."

"You mean we can keep her as a pet, Gran?" Tim asked excitedly.

"Maybe, Tim." Gran sighed sadly and exchanged a look with the park rangers. Tim could tell the grown-ups were upset.

"But that would be great, wouldn't it?" he asked, looking at all the adults. "It would be a lot better than if it died!"

Gran set the panther down in a leaf-lined cardboard box that one of the assistants had brought in for the cubs.

"You're right there, Tim. It *would* be better than her dying — better for her, and better for us. But it wouldn't help the species much. Florida panthers are meant to be wild and free, not kept as pets."

Gran picked up the other panther and pressed its belly. "Internal organs seem okay," she murmured, placing her stethoscope on the little creature's chest. "But the heartbeat is weak. I'm afraid we may lose this one."

Arden was horrified. "You mean he's going to die?" she blurted out, her voice cracking.

Gran's face softened, but her eyes still looked sad. "Let me put it this way — he doesn't have much chance without his mother."

"Oh." Arden looked crushed.

"But then," Gran went on, putting an arm around the girl's shoulder, "I've seen lots of cases that surprised me. Maybe this'll be one of them. Maybe with some good care, and a little luck, he'll pull through and I'll have to eat my words. I sure would love that."

Arden looked relieved. "Oh, Gran, can I hold him?"

"Yes, but you've got to be very gentle. Here, hold him close so he doesn't lose any body heat. And Pete, can we get to the chopper right away, please? I want these two under heat lamps as soon as possible."

"Let's go," said the ranger.

"Tim, you carry the female," Gran instructed. Then, turning to the rangers, she said, "Well, everyone, we'll let you know how they do."

With a quick good-bye, Gran and Tim and Arden got into the airboat. Soon they were back at the heliport, and then air-borne again. This time, Tim and Arden completely missed the splendor of the scene below them. They were too wrapped up in their new baby animal companions.

"Why is her head bobbing around like

that?" Tim asked as the tiny cub wriggled on his lap.

"I think she may be hungry," Gran answered. "Try giving her a bottle of that kitten milk replacement the rangers gave us. A little KMR should do the trick."

Sure enough, within minutes the panther had nursed herself full and fallen asleep on Tim's lap. *Look at her*, Tim thought. *Her face is all mushed up, but she's so cute.*

Tim had to laugh at himself. Here he was, playing mama to a furry little animal orphan, and loving every minute of it! Of course, what made it so exciting was the knowledge that someday the little pussycat in his arms would grow up to be one of the fiercest creatures on earth!

The panther Arden was holding sat listlessly in her lap. Arden stroked him gently on the head, but the little cub hardly responded. And when she offered him a bottle, he turned his head away.

"You must be wondering where you are and what's going on," Arden cooed to the tiny creature. "Maybe that's why you're not eating. But just you wait. When we get you back to River Oaks, we're going to take such good care of you that you'll grow up big and healthy — "

The little cub turned its head in the direction of her voice. "There!" cried Arden. "That's the spirit!" Then she got an idea. "Gran! Can I name him?" she asked.

"Well, I don't see why not," Gran replied.

"Then I'm naming him Spirit. 'Cause he's going to need a fighting spirit to survive."

Gran smiled warmly but didn't say anything. Tim could tell she didn't want to discourage Arden.

"I'm going to call mine Tawny," Tim announced, "for the color of her coat."

"Well, well — Spirit and Tawny," said Gran. "I hope you two like it at River Oaks."

Chapter Five

— • —

The Cubs Come Home

"It's them!"

Jesse had been waiting for the chopper for over twenty minutes. When he saw the big machine landing, he started jumping up and down beside his grandfather. "Tim! Arden!" he cried.

Jesse's eyes grew big as he watched his brother and sister step off the helicopter. They were carrying something — something alive! Jesse raced over to get a better look. "Wow!" he shouted when he saw the tiny creatures up close. "What are they, Gran?"

"They're Florida panthers, a type of mountain lion," Gran told him. "We couldn't save their mother. That's why we brought them here to River Oaks."

"Can I hold one?" asked Jesse, looking from Tim to Arden.

Arden shook her head. "Not this one. He's sick."

"Having a lot of people handle them isn't too good, Jess," Tim explained. "Maybe later, after they've gotten to know you or something."

"Hello, Tansy." Gramp threw an arm around Gran's shoulders and led the family to the waiting car. "Jesse and I have some news of our own. We picked up that dog from the mayor. She's got a nasty-looking cut on her left front leg. But other than that she looks okay."

"She looks more than okay," Jesse protested. "She looks *beautiful!* And she's really nice, too. We're gonna call her Ginger."

"I don't think she'll be with us very long, though," Gramp said. "She's a pure-bred setter," he explained. "But for now, at least, I guess we have three more mouths to feed."

"Oh, Thomas, I'm not sure the panthers are going to make it," Gran told Gramp in a soft voice that only Tim overheard. "They may just be too young."

"Well, it looks like they're doing fine right now," Gramp said, holding the door open for Tim and Arden.

"Normally I'd say they should go to the recovery barn, but it's kind of crowded there these days," Gran was saying. "I think we should get these two a big nesting box and keep it right on the back porch until they're a little older and we decide what to do with them."

Arden's face lit up with a smile. "You mean Spirit and Tawny can stay with us at home? Hooray!"

"I'll get a box right away," said Gramp, hopping out of the car. "Jesse, I'll need some help carrying it. It's not very heavy, but it's bulky."

"Let's show our little orphans their new home," Gran said, leading Tim and Arden onto the screened porch at the back of the house. "This is a good place for them," she went on. "It's protected, but it still has the feel of outdoors."

"Here we come!" shouted Gramp through the kitchen door. He and Jesse were carrying a big box made from corrugated cardboard. It was about six feet square.

"Since we want the little critters to feel at home," Gramp said, setting the box down, "Jesse and I covered the bottom with straw. Blankets might be softer," he added, "but this is a lot closer to the way it is in the wild."

Both panthers slept soundly while their new habitat was being assembled. That was normal, Gran explained. Like human babies, they would sleep up to sixteen hours a day at first.

Tim and Arden sat patiently, the cubs on their laps. "Okay, Sport, let's go get the heat lamps," Gramp said to Jesse.

"Arden, has Spirit taken any KMR yet?" Gran asked gently, glancing down at the full bottle her granddaughter was holding.

"Not yet," Arden replied. She could tell Gran was worried about Spirit.

"Well, maybe after they get settled . . . " said Gran.

Arden tenderly stroked Spirit's back. The little cub was so soft and warm in her lap. He couldn't die. He just couldn't!

"Hey! Tawny's chewing my finger!" Tim piped up. "She was sleeping, and then, wham! It's a good thing she doesn't have any teeth!"

"They won't come in for a few weeks at least," said Gran with an amused smile. "Tawny's pretty frisky for a girl who just took a big trip."

"Here we go," said Gramp, coming in and setting up the lamps. They cast a warm glow in the nesting box. "Nice and toasty. I just wish the light wasn't so bright."

"I know!" said Arden. "The rangers said they found the cubs' den in a group of gumbo-limbo trees. We could put some gumbo-limbo leaves in the box, and hang some branches over it, under the heat lamps."

"Arden, that's a great idea! You've really got a talent for this kind of work," said Gran.

Gramp winked, adding, "Of course she does! She's a Quinn. She comes by it naturally."

The gumbo-limbo branches were perfect. They filtered the light into warm shadows — shadows that would be familiar to the two tiny creatures wriggling in Tim's and Arden's laps.

"I wish I could hold one of them, just for a minute," Jesse said wistfully.

Arden just shook her head, and so did Tim. The cubs were their responsibility now, and they both knew it was too soon for the little creatures to be handed around.

"Sorry, Jesse," said Tim as he placed the bottle of KMR alongside Tawny's cheek. The infant panther turned her head and eagerly bit at the nipple, tugging and pulling on it till she'd guzzled the last drop. Then she fell back onto Tim's lap, purring contentedly. Her tiny paws grasped and released Tim's corduroy slacks over and over again.

"She's going back to sleep, I bet," Tim whispered, gently placing the baby in the nesting box.

Spirit seemed only half awake. The sickly cub managed to drink a bit of KMR Arden fed him with a medicine dropper. "Go ahead and get some rest," she said, laying him down next to his sister.

In the box, the groggy little panther orphans found each other. In seconds, they had curled up together and were breathing quietly. The Quinns all tiptoed from the room. Even Ginger limped out quietly.

That night, after dinner, Jesse finally got his chance to hold Tawny.

"Here, like this," said Tim, demonstrating the proper way to hold the tiny cub. "Not too tight. And make sure her feet are supported."

Jesse broke into a warm grin. "She's purring! Listen!" The little cub sounded like a motorboat.

"There, that's the way," Tim said. "See? She likes you! She likes people!"

Jesse put Tawny back in her box and then turned toward the other cub. "Uh-oh!" he cried. "What's that white blob by Spirit?"

Arden jumped up to take a look. "Oh, no! He spit up his milk," she moaned, cleaning the box with a paper towel.

Arden hated to even think of it, but she knew Spirit wasn't doing as well as Tawny. He had spit up the little KMR he had drunk, and from the look on Gran's face, Arden could tell that wasn't a good sign.

"What about tonight?" Arden asked Tim after Jesse had gone up to bed. "Gran said the cubs have to feed every couple of hours or so."

Tim thought about that for a minute.

"Tell you what," he said. "We can take turns sleeping and nursing."

"Okay," said Arden. "I'll take the first shift."

They both looked down at the panther orphans in the box. Their tiny stomachs were rising and falling peacefully. Arden and Tim looked at each other and couldn't help smiling. "The big cats, huh?" said Arden with a little giggle.

"Well, they will be — someday," Tim said. He hoped that day wouldn't come *too* soon, though. He liked Tawny exactly the way she was.

Just then, Gran came out, her medical bag in hand and her stethoscope hanging from her neck.

"How're we doing, kids?" she asked, crouching down beside them.

"Good, Gran," said Arden. "Tim and I decided to take turns looking after the cubs tonight."

Gran looked surprised but pleased. "Well!" she laughed. "You're real Quinns, the two of you!" And she proudly patted them both on the back. "Now before I turn in, I want to have a look at the patients."

Tansy Quinn carefully lifted Spirit from the box and listened to the tiny heartbeat. "Mmmm . . . " she said.

Arden couldn't tell what that meant. "How's he doing, Gran?" she asked.

"About the same," said Gran as she put the cub back down. "We'll see what tomorrow brings. But he's got to start eating soon. . . ." Her voice drifted off. "Well," she said, reaching in for the other cub, "let's have a look at *you*."

Very gently, she lifted Tawny up by the scruff of the neck. The little animal yawned and squinted one eye open. "That's good," said Gran, nodding as she listened to Tawny's heart. "You're coming along nicely."

Gran stood up and took off her stethoscope. "I'm off to bed, " she said. "Your sleeping bags are right behind the chair there," she told her grandchildren. "Good night."

" 'Night, Gran."

"Good night, Gran."

Alone again, Tim and Arden were silent for a long time. Tim could tell his sister was upset.

"Don't look so sad," he told her. "Spirit hasn't begun to fight yet. And neither have we!"

"You're right," Arden said. "I guess I'll try some KMR one more time before bed," she said, getting up to go to the kitchen.

"Bring some for Tawny, too, okay?" Tim called after her. *Poor Arden*, he thought. He hoped she wouldn't take it too hard if Spirit didn't make it.

Tim looked up at the place where he and Arden had patched the screen with cardboard. "What about this?" he asked when Arden returned.

"Don't worry," she answered. "I don't think they could possibly crawl out of that hole, do you? It's so high up, and they can barely walk."

"I suppose you're right," Tim yawned.

45

"But let's remember to fix it soon, okay?"

Both youngsters began feeding their cubs. Once more, Tawny gobbled down her formula. Tim could almost feel the weight she'd gained, just in one day!

In no time, Tawny had drained the bottle. But Arden was still trying to get Spirit to take the nipple. "Come on,

Spirit," she coaxed. "Just one sip, okay? Please. . . ?" Suddenly Arden stopped talking and a big smile lit up her face. Spirit had finally grabbed the nipple and was pulling away on it! For about a minute, time seemed to stand still. Then the cub released his hold and went instantly back to sleep.

"Did you see that?" Arden whispered from across the porch. "Did you?"

Tim nodded. "I told you, Arden," he said. "Spirit'll come through, you'll see."

Giggling, Arden brought Spirit over to the nesting box. As she passed Tim, she held up the dropper. It was empty. "Great!" Tim said.

Back in their box, the little cubs stumbled around. Then they flopped down and began crawling all over each other, trying to get comfortable.

Tim and Arden had to laugh — the cubs were so adorable. Tim looked over at his sister. "This must be the way parents feel," he whispered.

Arden nodded, still looking at the

cubs. "Mom and Dad loved us just like this," she said.

And they still do, Tim thought contentedly, picturing his parents in far-off Africa. *And they always will, too.*

Chapter Six

——•——

Missing!

The next week flew by for Tim and Arden. Every day they took Tawny and Spirit outside so the cubs could romp in the grass. The orphans were still weak on their feet, so they did a lot more stumbling than romping. It was good exercise, though, and tons of fun for everyone.

Sometimes the Irish setter, Ginger, would join them. She'd hover over the little cats, acting more like a mother hen than a dog. The cubs seemed to accept her as a friend.

Tawny seemed always full of energy, ready for food every few hours, and always eager to explore the world around her.

And Spirit was doing better. He seemed a little livelier and stronger with each passing day. True, he spit up at least half of the KMR Arden gave him, but at least he was nursing regularly now. That in itself was a victory.

One afternoon, Tim was out on the lawn with Tawny when Arden came hurrying over. "Tim!" she said, "Gran wanted to see the cubs in the infirmary this morning! She's been waiting for us. Bring Tawny right away, and I'll get Spirit!"

"I forgot!" answered Tim, scooping Tawny up gently under his arm and hurrying to the infirmary.

When they'd first taken the panthers from Everglades Park, Gran had agreed to keep close tabs on their development. Since Spirit and Tawny were endangered animals, she had to fill out lots of reports about them. That meant the cubs had to be given formal exams every two weeks.

"Hi, Gran, sorry I'm late," said Tim, hurrying into the infirmary.

Gran looked up at the black-and-white clock on her office wall. "It's okay. I know you were having a good time with Tawny, and that counts," she said.

Tim followed his grandmother into the examining room and set Tawny down on the long metal table. "I have to take a blood count today," Gran murmured, taking out a needle.

The little panther flinched, and then it was over. Gran capped the glass tube filled with bright red blood and labeled it. "Okay, now it's Spirit's turn. Where is he?" Just then Arden appeared with the little cub.

"Come in," said Gran. "Join the party."

As soon as Spirit's blood count had been taken, Gran weighed both cubs. Tawny had gained three and a half ounces — but Spirit had put on just half an ounce.

"Well, at least he didn't lose," Gran murmured, trying to sound hopeful. "That's something."

51

After the cubs had been examined, Gran turned to Tim and Arden. "Meet me in the office, kids. I want to talk to you."

Arden and Tim exchanged a look. Gran sounded so serious. She wasn't going to say the cubs had to leave River Oaks, was she? Gathering Spirit and Tawny up, they went into the office and waited nervously.

At last Gran appeared. She took a seat in the old leather chair behind her desk. "Tim, Arden, I want to start by saying how very proud I am of the work you've been doing with these two panthers. Two weeks ago, I wouldn't have given either Tawny or Spirit much chance for survival. But today they both show weight gain, and they're obviously on the right track. I'm sure their progress is due to all the care and attention you've given them."

Tim was grinning from ear to ear, and so was Arden. "You mean they're going to live, Gran?" asked Arden.

Gran gave Arden a serious look. "I'm almost certain Tawny will survive, but I can't really say about Spirit. Medically, he's got some serious problems. By rights, he shouldn't be alive today, and yet, here he is."

They all looked at the little cub waddling across the floor, and laughed.

"Gran, Spirit *is* going to survive,"

Arden declared, picking up the little cub and stroking him under the chin. And with that, he broke out purring so loudly they could all hear it.

"Well, he certainly seems to agree with you," Gran laughed. But then her expression grew serious again as she said, "If the cubs keep improving the way they have been, I'm thinking of trying to return them to the wild as soon as possible. I believe they'd have an excellent chance of survival — especially Tawny — given the proper training."

Tim knew he should be happy, but he wasn't. "But Gran," he said, "when the cubs first came here, you said they could be pets."

"You're right, Tim, I did say that. But that was because I never expected them to do so well here at River Oaks."

"How would we train them for the wild, Gran?" asked Arden. "Teach them to hunt?"

"Well, that's a big question. I don't

know if we should even discuss it till we're sure they . . . well, not for a while yet. Right now, nursing is the most important thing. We've got to keep them strong and healthy until they're a little older."

"Tawny eats better if I hold her in my lap," said Tim.

Gran nodded and bit her lip. "That's good, Tim. Tawny needs that closeness as long as she's nursing. But if we do decide to return her to the wild, you'll have to back off some. An animal can't survive in the wild unless it can recognize its greatest enemy. . . ."

Tim wore a puzzled look until Gran explained. "A Florida panther's greatest enemy is man," she said. "Eventually Tawny and Spirit will have to learn to distrust people — starting with you."

"What?" Tim cried. "But Gran, I — "

"Listen, maybe I shouldn't have said anything yet," Gran interrupted. "But I wanted to warn you not to get *too* close to the cubs — for their sakes. When we're dealing with infant wildlife, we have to be very careful. Anyway, we'll cross that bridge when we come to it — *if* we come to it. I want to talk the whole situation over with some other people in the Panther Recovery Program. The kind of return I'm thinking about may not even be possible."

Gran glanced up at the clock. "I have to go meet a farmer about a calf now," she said. "But I wanted you to know how proud of you I am. Tell Gramp to start supper without me, okay? I should be back before seven," she added as she hurried out the door.

Walking back to the house, Arden and Tim were quiet as they thought over what Gran had said.

Tim held Tawny tightly to his chest. Did Gran mean he shouldn't be friends with Tawny anymore? he wondered. No, he decided. She couldn't have meant *that*. Or could she. . . ?

As if to mirror Tim's worries, the day suddenly began to darken. Black clouds blew across the sky, driven by a rising wind.

"It's going to storm," Arden said. "We'd better get the cubs back inside!"

Tim nodded, and together the two children crossed the yard to the back porch, huddling over the little panthers to protect them from the wind.

* * *

Dear Mom and Dad. . . .

Tim sat at the desk in his bedroom, listening to the wind howl outside. Big bolts of lightning went off every few seconds, like giant flashbulbs, followed by great crashes of thunder that made the windows rattle. Above the sound of the pouring rain, he heard Ginger barking nervously and Jesse telling her to be quiet. With all that going on, it was almost impossible to write.

Still, Tim was eager to get this letter off to his parents. He was glad he'd never sent the other one complaining about life at River Oaks. So much had happened since then. . . .

Dear Mom and Dad,
I have a great new project — Arden and I are rearing two baby Florida panthers! Mine is named Tawny, and she's so cute it's incredible. I always wanted to work with fierce wild animals, and it's really neat to think that someday Tawny will be one of them. Right now she's no bigger than a puppy —

A loud clap of thunder startled Tim. Tawny and Spirit must be scared down there, he thought, putting down his pen and dashing out the door.

He bumped into Arden at the bottom of the stairs. "Are you thinking what I'm thinking?" she asked.

Tim nodded, and together they ran to

the back porch, pursued by Ginger, who was barking her head off. Suddenly a huge streak of lightning lit up the sky, shortly followed by an earsplitting thunderclap. "The storm's right over us!" Tim cried out, opening the porch door. "Tawny!" he called.

In the box the little cub lay huddled under a bunch of leaves. "She's hiding!" Tim said, his voice full of relief.

"What about Spirit?" Arden sounded frantic as she rummaged through the leaves in the box. "He's gone!" she cried. "But where could he go? There's no way off the porch — "

The minute the words were out of her mouth, Arden realized they weren't true. Tim must have been thinking the same thing, because he looked over at the torn screen just as Arden did. The cardboard had been blown away, and the little tear in the screen was now a big gash. In his panic, the sickly little cub had somehow managed to climb the gumbo-limbo branches and tear his way through the screen!

"Spirit!" cried Arden. "He's out there in the storm!"

"Come on!" yelled Tim. "We've got to find him — there's no time to lose!"

Chapter Seven

———•———

Out in the Storm

"Don't worry, Arden. He can't have gone far!"

Tim grabbed hold of his sister's hand, but Arden just stood there, a dazed look in her eyes. Ginger was already by the door, waiting to run outside.

"It's all my fault," Arden murmured. "Poor Spirit. How could I have let him down like this?"

Tim shook her gently. "Look it's not anybody's fault. It just happened, that's all. Now, where do Gran and Gramp keep the flashlights?"

"On the shelf in the pantry."

"You get our raincoats, and I'll get

the flashlights," said Tim on his way out of the room.

"Let's not tell Jesse or Gran or Gramp what's happening. Not till we find Spirit," said Arden, brushing away a tear.

"Okay. Meet me back here in two minutes," said Tim.

By the time they had the rain gear and the flashlights ready, the thunder and lightning had passed. But the rain was still falling in sheets, making the night seem darker than usual.

Arden and Tim stepped out into the furious storm with Ginger at their heels. "He's probably right near the porch," said Tim. Hopefully, he searched the palmetto bushes that grew around the house — but no Spirit.

"Spirit!" Arden called, her face lashed by the wind and rain.

"If he was on the lawn, we'd see him," Tim said, looking over the backyard. "Hey! Look at Ginger!"

The Irish setter was sniffing at some

palmetto bushes. Suddenly she turned toward a small stand of cedar and gumbo-limbo trees on the other side of the lawn and began barking furiously.

"Right, Ginger!" cried Arden. "I bet that's more like Spirit's home in the wild than anything else at River Oaks!"

"Let's go," shouted Tim. As he ran across the lawn, gusts of wind buffeted him. The storm was blowing across the lawn right at them. Arden had to put her elbows up to protect her face from the wildly swaying branches and the stinging rain.

Entering the sheltered area, they began calling Spirit's name. They searched every inch of the little thicket. But in the end, even Ginger seemed to give up.

"It's all my fault, Tim," Arden said again, plopping herself miserably down on a fallen tree limb. "Gramp wanted to fix that screen when we were leaving for the picnic, and I told him not to bother! And then *you* wondered if we should fix it when the cubs first got here, and I said it would be okay. Then I forgot all about it — and now look what happened! I'm so mad I could spit!"

Tim hated to see his sister so upset. "Arden," he said gently, "we *all* forgot about that tear in the screen — not just you. Anyway, what's important isn't who's to blame, it's finding Spirit! Come on, we can't give up yet!"

Just then Ginger started sniffing at a spot on the ground and wagging her tail.

"What? What is it, girl?" said Arden, jumping up and running after Ginger. The dog led them through a wild growth of thorns. Arden and Tim got scratched all over their arms, but they were so excited they barely noticed. Sure enough, in the middle of the whole tangle, huddled next to an enormous gumbo-limbo trunk, was Spirit!

"He's here! He's here!" Arden cried. She swept the baby panther up into her arms and tucked him under her raincoat.

"Gosh, he's cold," she murmured, wrapping a scarf around the shivering cub. The rain had soaked Spirit's fur, and Tim could make out every one of his ribs.

But skinny or not, Spirit was alive! "I can't believe we found him," Arden kept saying over and over. "Good old Ginger — "

"Arden! Tim!" Tansy Quinn's voice sounded small in the rain from so far away.

The kids turned and saw their grandmother standing by the porch door, a worried frown on her face.

"Come on, Tim, let's get back to the house," said Arden. "We're here, Gran!" she yelled as they emerged from the thicket and went dashing across the lawn.

Gran held the door open for the rain-drenched group. "What in the world's going on?" she asked. "What happened to the screen? And where's Spirit?"

"Here he is, Gran!" said Arden, producing the panther from under her coat.

"We came down to check on the cubs, and he was gone!"

"He must have climbed up the branches we put in front of the heat lamps," said Tim breathlessly.

Gran took the little panther into her strong, steady hands. "Hmmm . . ." she murmured.

"Is he okay?" Arden asked.

"Feel the tips of his ears," said Gran.

Arden did. They were burning hot.

"Oh, no!" she moaned. "And it's all because I didn't care about the rip in the screen!"

"Arden, he does have a fever," said Gran. "And I'm sure being out there in the rain didn't help. But I believe the fever is from something else."

Gran put the panther gently into Arden's arms and sat her granddaughter down. "Arden," she said, "I have a confession to make. I haven't been quite honest with you about Spirit. You've been doing such a wonderful job caring for him that I didn't want to discourage you in any way. But the truth is, I've known all along that Spirit has a serious eating disorder. All the signs are there: spitting up, the lack of weight gain, and most of all, this. . . . Here, Arden, feel this spot under his belly."

Arden slipped her fingers beneath the little cub's stomach and felt a hard lump. "But that's just a bone," she said. "What's wrong with that?"

"It's as hard as bone," Gran said, "but there shouldn't be any bones there. I strongly suspect that lump is undigested KMR. Spirit wouldn't be the first wild cub who couldn't adjust to man-made food. It's a fairly common problem with wild creatures who are deprived of their mother's milk."

Arden looked as if she was going to cry. "But still," she whispered, "I should have taken better care of him. It's all my fault. I — "

"Stop blaming yourself, Arden," said

Gran. "Without the eating disorder, Spirit would have had no trouble at all being out in a rainstorm. That's not why he's dying. . . ."

Dying? Arden could hardly believe what Gran was saying. "But Gran," she cried, "can't we do anything about it? Can't we just give Spirit something else to eat?"

"I'm afraid not. Scientists are searching for better and better milk replacements all the time, but they haven't come up with anything yet. I'm so sorry, Arden. I know how much you love Spirit."

"I won't let him die, Gran!" Arden declared. "I won't! I'll do anything! I'll stay up all night! I'll stay by him every second — "

Gran put her arm around her granddaughter's shoulders as Arden burst into tears. "Arden," she said, "what we need here is a miracle. They happen sometimes, I know they do, and I'm going to hope for one now.

"But if he doesn't survive, you've got to understand that it had nothing to do with you. Losing Spirit would be nature's decision, not ours. Nature can seem harsh sometimes, but we've got to trust in it — even if we can't always understand. We're a part of it ourselves, you know."

"Okay, Gran," Arden gulped.

"Are you all right now, honey?" asked Gran, standing up.

"I think so," answered Arden.

"Well, we'll leave you alone then. Come on, Tim. Arden, we'll see you in the morning. But be sure to wake me if you need anything during the night."

"I'll be okay. Thanks, Gran."

Gran squeezed Arden's hand and then led Tim quietly from the room, leaving the girl and the cub alone together.

When Tim opened his eyes the next morning, the house was quieter than usual. He knew right away what had happened during the night. He could sense it in the air.

Walking into the kitchen for breakfast, he saw Gran, Gramp, and Jesse seated quietly around the big wooden table. There were plates of untouched food in front of them.

"Tim . . . 'morning . . . " Gramp murmured. Gramp was trying to smile, but he wasn't having much success.

"Where's Arden?" Tim asked, not wanting to hear the answer.

"She's in her room," said Gran. "Tim, last night. . . ."

Here it was. Tim braced himself and then finished Gran's sentence for her. "Spirit died."

A silent nod answered him.

Dazed, Tim sat down at the table, but he waved Gran away when she tried to put a plate in front of him.

"It wasn't anyone's fault, Tim. The cub had an eating disorder and there was nothing any of us could do. It's amazing that he survived as long as he did," Gran explained.

"How's Arden doing?" asked Tim.

"Not very well," Gran answered. "I think it would help if you went up and talked to her."

Tim nodded, and frowned thoughtfully. It wouldn't be easy, talking to Arden. He wasn't sure he knew what to say. Still, his sister needed him.

With a mumbled "Excuse me," Tim got up from the table and made his way to Arden's room.

She was lying in bed, her head buried under her pillow.

Tim sat on the edge of the bed and leaned over. "Arden?" he said very softly. "It's me. Tim."

"Go away," came the muffled answer. "I don't want to talk to anybody."

"You just listen, Arden. I want to say something. Okay?" He waited, but she didn't answer, so he went on.

"Remember the night Spirit's mother died? Remember how they found Spirit and Tawny right away? We didn't even have a chance to be sad, did we? And it was so horrible, the way their mom had to die. . . .

"See, we didn't really get to cry about it then. Her babies needed us, and we went to them. We knew what we would feel like if . . . you know, if *our* parents. . . .

"Well, now you've got time to cry, and it's okay. It's only right. But just remember one thing, Arden. We still have one cub left. We've still got Tawny. And she's going to make it, I promise you that. I *promise* you that."

Arden poked her head out from under the pillow. Her eyes were red and puffy from crying.

"But what am *I* supposed to do now?" she whispered. "There's nothing I can do for Tawny. And it's too late for Spirit." The tears were rising in her eyes again.

"I bet I know an animal you can still do something for — one who's been missing you an awful lot lately," Tim said.

Arden bit her lip. "Glory!" she said, sitting up a little straighter on the bed. "Gosh, I really have been ignoring her these past few weeks. She must think I don't care about her anymore."

"Spirit needed you, Arden. I wouldn't be surprised if Glory understands that somehow."

"You really think so, Tim?" Arden tilted her head to one side. "I hope you're right."

"Arden, remember when Mom and Dad first told us about River Oaks and how not all the animals make it?"

"Uh–huh." Arden nodded.

"Well, they were right. And it really hurts to lose one. But they also said we've got to keep going, caring for the ones who do make it, remember?"

"Like Glory. . . ." Arden narrowed her dark eyes thoughtfully. "Maybe I'll go down to the stable," she finally said. "I won't ever forget Spirit, but right now I think I want to be with Glory for a while."

With a sigh, Arden swung her legs over the side of the bed. "Thanks, Tim," she said, managing a small smile. "You know, you're a pretty great brother."

"Aw," said Tim, embarrassed, "forget about it, okay? You're pretty great yourself," he added, giving her a big hug.

Chapter Eight

———•———

Back to Nature

Tim woke up in the middle of the night. He guessed he'd been having a bad dream. Looking at the alarm clock, he saw that it was three-thirty A.M. Almost time to get up for Tawny's feeding. He still had to nurse her once in the middle of the night.

Tim reached over to turn off the alarm and pulled himself out of bed. Yawning, he put on his robe and went to the kitchen for Tawny's bottle. He heated it up and walked out onto the porch.

He expected to find Tawny waiting to welcome him as usual. But tonight she was huddled in a corner of the box, curled up in a little ball. Her golden eyes were wide open, and she seemed to be staring at the side of the nesting box without really seeing it.

"Hey, Tawny — hi, girl," said Tim when he walked in. That was all he'd ever had to say to bring her running to the edge of the box, looking for her bottle. But not tonight. Tonight she just turned her head and looked up at him sadly.

She misses Spirit, just like we do, Tim realized. Tawny and Spirit had been such great partners — playing together, sleeping together.

"Come on, girl, time for some milk," said Tim, gently picking up the little panther and placing her in his lap. Usually Tawny would break out purring at the first touch, but tonight she was silent.

"Here you go, Tawny," whispered Tim, placing the nipple by the panther's mouth. Tawny turned her head away.

"Not hungry?" said Tim. "But you hardly had a thing before. Why don't you give it a try?"

Again, the cub turned away from the

nipple. There was no sense forcing her, so Tim gently laid Tawny back in the box.

"You miss Spirit, huh? I understand. Well, I'll see you later, then," he said, before walking back to the kitchen and putting the KMR away.

On the way back to his room, Tim stopped by Arden's door. He opened it quietly so he wouldn't wake his sister. On Arden's bureau was a drawing of Spirit, which Tim had given her earlier that night. When she'd seen it, Arden had burst out crying again. Next to the picture was a little vase filled with wild-flowers.

Even in sleep, Arden looked sad. Tim closed the door softly and returned to his own room.

Lying in bed, he had an awful thought. *What if it had been Tawny who died?* Tim wasn't sure he could have taken that.

He glanced at the clock — five after four. Maybe he should try to feed Tawny one more time.

Tiptoeing out of bed, he made the same trip to the porch. Again Tawny was awake. Again, she refused to feed.

By the time Tim was back in bed, the sky was beginning to lighten. *What if Tawny dies of a broken heart?* Tim wondered. It could happen. According to Gran, animals had been known to fail when their caretakers turned on them or abandoned them. It was only natural.

At five-thirty the sun rose over River Oaks, bursting through the thin clouds like a bright yellow sword.

Restless again, Tim went to find Tawny, a bottle of KMR in hand. "Come on, Tawny," he cooed, settling the cub in his lap. "Come on, girl. I know it hurts, but you've got to keep going. You have your whole life ahead of you."

This time, Tim finally got through. When he placed the nipple against the cub's mouth, Tawny began sucking away. *Thank goodness*, thought Tim, relaxing onto the old swing that Gran and Gramp kept on the porch.

Tawny finished that bottle and part of another one. Then the boy and the panther cuddled up together. Tawny purred contentedly as Tim stroked her back. Soon they both were fast asleep. Gran and Gramp found them there at about seven-thirty.

"Well, I'll be," said Gramp, gently shaking Tim awake. "Tansy, this boy's going to be a real 'animals man' yet!"

"Could be," laughed Gran, as a sleepy Tim rubbed his eyes. "But I'll tell you one thing for sure: Because of Tim, that little cub is going to make it."

Two weeks later when Tim and Tawny were out playing on the lawn, Jesse joined them. He was carrying a hamburger.

"Hi, Tim," Jesse said. "What are you doing?"

"Teaching Tawny some tricks," Tim answered. "Here, look at this." Jesse watched Tim move his hand as if it were a tail, waving his fingers in the grass in front of Tawny. The little panther dropped her belly to the ground and fixed her eyes on Tim's wiggling hand. Then she snuck up closer and pounced on it in a flash!

"Good girl!" Tim said, ruffling the cub's ears affectionately.

"That's great!" said Jesse with a big smile.

"And that's not all she can do," Tim said proudly. "She can play a mean game of 'Chew,' too. Look." Tim stretched his arm out in front of the little panther, who grabbed onto it and began gnawing away.

Tim winced and pulled his arm back. "Maybe that's not such a good game anymore. She's getting teeth. It's okay, girl," he told the panther, stroking her fur. "I know you didn't mean to hurt me."

"Can I pet her?" Jesse asked, leaning down toward the little cub. "Hey!" he yelled suddenly. "She's stealing my 'burger!"

Tim and Jesse laughed. Tawny had torn off a big chunk of Jesse's hamburger and was greedily gobbling it up.

"Hey, that's my lunch!" Jesse teased.

"It's the first time she's ever taken any meat," said Tim.

"Well, she sure seems to like it!" laughed Jesse.

The sudden sound of hoofbeats turned the boys' attention away from Tawny. They waved as Arden and Glory came riding up the path. By the time they looked back at the panther cub, there was no sign at all of Jesse's hamburger.

"Tawny looks great, Tim," said Arden, reining in beside her brother. "You must be brushing her a lot. Her coat is so shiny."

"Thanks," Tim replied with a smile. "But she doesn't need me to brush her. That's just the way her coat is. Glory looks good, too."

It was hard to believe that this healthy, sleek thoroughbred was the same mangy, beaten, half-starved filly Gramp had saved from the slaughterhouse not so long ago.

Tim's eyes met Arden's, and Tim could tell they were both thinking about

Spirit. But neither of them said anything.

"Gran told me she's seeing Tawny in the infirmary," Arden finally said.

"Yup," said Tim. "Today's her big checkup."

Jesse suddenly remembered something. "Oh, by the way, Gramp says anybody who wants a hamburger should go in and get one," he said.

"Okay. Thanks, Jess," said Arden. "You coming, Tim?"

"Not yet. I'll wait till after Tawny sees Gran. She's got her one-month examination today," Tim explained. "In fact, I'd better get right over there. See you later."

He scooped up the little panther. By now Tawny was used to riding in his arms. Together, they made their way to the infirmary, where Gran was waiting for them.

"Hi, Tim, come on in," she said. "I see Tawny looks good. Let's run a few tests."

While Gran weighed the little cub, Tim told her all about Tawny's latest accomplishments.

"I think she's getting over losing Spirit," he said. "Those first few days, she was kind of moping around. I figured she needed a playmate, so I started pretending I was a little panther, too. And it really worked. She's a great pouncer."

"Well, I hope those marks on your arms didn't come from Tawny," Gran said, with a look of concern.

Tim had forgotten about the scratches. "Oh," he said, dropping his arms to his sides. "They're nothing. Hey! And guess what, Gran! Tawny ate some of Jesse's hamburger! She just pulled it right out of his hand. You should have seen her. She was so funny."

Tim was smiling from ear to ear, but Gran suddenly turned serious. "Is something the matter, Gran?" he asked her.

"No, not really, Tim. It's just that . . . well . . . remember a while back I told you I was considering training Tawny to go back into the wild?"

"Sure, I remember," Tim replied nervously.

"Well, we've decided to try it."

"But Gran, I was thinking, if Tawny goes back to where her mother lived, she might get killed, too!"

"That's a chance we have to take,

Tim," Gran said. "Tawny doesn't belong to us, remember? She belongs to the wild."

Tim gulped. It was true, and he knew it. "Okay, Gran. When do we start?"

"The sooner the better. As of tomorrow, everything will have to change."

Tim looked down at the cub on his lap.

"For starters," Gran went on, "no more bottles or nursing — no hand-feeding of any sort. Tawny's got to learn that she can't depend on us for her food anymore. She'll have to learn how to find it and kill it herself."

"But that will take time, Gran. We'll still feed her till she can take care of herself, won't we?"

"Yes, we will, Tim. But she doesn't have to know that. We can use a blind box. Gramp will show you how."

Tim looked up at his grandmother as if she were speaking a foreign language.

"And of course," Gran went on, "we'll

have to change her habitat. I've asked Gramp to start fencing off five acres for Tawny's use. I'd like Ginger to stay in there with her a few hours a day. Just for a while, of course, to help her get adjusted."

"Wait a minute," cried Tim, his head spinning. "Why Ginger? What's Ginger got to do with this?"

"Well, Tim, Ginger can be a connection for Tawny — a bridge from civilization back to the wild. She can give Tawny the contact she needs, without the help of a human. Right now, the most important thing for Tawny is cutting all ties to humans. People are her biggest enemy in nature and she has to learn to distrust them."

"Even *me*?" asked Tim.

"I'm afraid so," Gran said. "After tomorrow, you're not to have any contact with her whatsoever. I know that may seem cruel, but I promise you, it's for the best."

Tim could hardly move. Every muscle in his body had turned to stone.

"She'll miss you at first," Gran said, "just like she missed Spirit. But remember, Tawny was born to live alone. She'll learn to adjust. And she'll also learn the most important lesson for a panther — that she can't count on humans, ever. Not even the good ones."

Tim was silent. He felt as if he'd been punched in the stomach.

"You understand, Tim? This is all for Tawny's own good," said Gran.

Tim knew she was trying to ease the blow, but it didn't help. "I understand," he lied. "I'd better get back, Gran. . . ." And he took Tawny in his arms and fled out of the infirmary.

Gran is the one who doesn't understand, he thought. *Tawny needs me!*

Chapter Nine

Letting Go

"Come on! We've got a ton of work to do." Gramp was already outside, holding the door open for Tim.

Tim gave Tawny one last stroke and put her down in her nesting box. "See you later, girl," he said.

"Where are we going?" Tim asked, hurrying to keep up with his grandfather.

"Down near the okapi habitat," Gramp said, without turning around. "We're going to finish making a territory for Tawny. We'll start off with five acres. Later, we'll add another fifteen. Panthers need lots of room to roam."

Tim put his head down and kept walking. Today they would finish the big fence, and tomorrow they'd put Tawny behind it. After that, Tim would never be able to hold his little cub again — never.

"Rudy has most of the fence up. We'll finish whatever's left and get to work on the blind box," said Gramp.

"How does a blind box work, Gramp?" Tim asked.

"You drop the meat into it. Then, your side of the box closes. Later, after you're gone, the animal's side opens. That way Tawny will have no trouble finding the food, but she won't know how it got there. We'll wear gloves, too, so she can't pick up our scent."

Tim winced. It all sounded so cold, so cruel. Nobody seemed to understand that Tawny loved him! He couldn't just let her down all of a sudden like that!

"But what if it doesn't work out?" Tim asked. "I mean, what if Tawny *doesn't* get used to being all alone like that?"

Thomas Quinn gave his grandson a worried look and threw an arm around his shoulder. "Tim," he said slowly, "it's important that this *does* work out. I want you to understand that. Tawny is not just any animal, you know. She's one of the last of a rare breed. I know it hurts to give her up, but sometimes we have to do the right thing, even if it breaks our heart."

Tim looked down at the ground. There was a coil of fencing, and a stack of long planks.

"Tim, you've done a great job with her up till now," Gramp went on. "But that's all over. After today, you mustn't even make eye contact with Tawny."

Tim was almost crying, but he refused to let the tears fall. "Won't Tawny think I'm not her friend anymore?" he asked.

"You *can't* be her friend anymore," Gramp answered, giving Tim's shoulder a squeeze. "That's the whole point. So if you want to say good-bye, do it today."

All that afternoon, Tim and Tawny were together. And all night long, Tim lay on a blanket on the porch floor, holding his little cub in his arms, not sleeping at all. He knew that in the morning it would all be over.

When daylight came, Tim carried Tawny out to the new enclosure. The little cub kept looking up at Tim with her huge yellow eyes. She seemed confused when he gave her one last hug, climbed the ladder, and dropped her gently down on the other side of the fence.

"Good-bye, girl. Good luck," said Tim, forcing himself to turn and walk away. He didn't look back, not even once. The time for looking was over. Tim swore to himself he would be strong.

But later that day, after lunch, when everyone was off doing chores, Tim stole down to the new habitat with a pair of binoculars in hand. He just wanted to see how Tawny was doing, all by herself.

And there she was, lying on a rock with the saddest expression on her face.

Tim couldn't bear the way she was just staring off into space like that. That's exactly how she'd looked after Spirit died, Tim remembered.

But this time Tawny was thinking of him — he knew it. Missing him, just as he was missing her.

It can't hurt to say hello, just this once, Tim told himself. He looked back to make sure there was nobody around. Then he walked up to the fence and called in a loud whisper, "Tawny! Here, girl!"

Instantly the little cub pricked up her ears and came running to Tim. He could hear her purring, even across the fence, and it made him feel good.

The chain-link fence had holes in it, holes as big around as a child's arm. Tim reached out to the baby panther and touched her back. She sidled up to the fence, leaning into it to get closer to Tim.

"How's it going in there, Tawny?" Tim asked. Her big golden eyes said "Lonely."

"Don't worry," Tim told her, "I haven't forgotten you. I — "

"Tim!"

Tim spun around guiltily at the sound of his name. His face was bright red, and his heart was beating wildly.

"Arden! What are you doing here? I thought you were with Glory."

Arden gave Tim a puzzled look. "Isn't today the day you were going to train Tawny for the wild?" she asked, knowing the answer was yes.

"Well, I — I figured since it was her first day she might be feeling lonely," Tim sputtered.

Arden shook her head sadly. "Tim, how can you go against everything Gran and Gramp said? Don't you trust them?"

"Sure, I do, but they just don't understand. Tawny needs me!"

Arden stared at her brother, while Tawny looked back and forth between them. Then the little panther began pawing at the fence.

"I'm going," Arden announced. "I don't want to hear anymore."

With a pained look, Tim turned back to Tawny. The panther was clearly upset now, clawing the fence and mewing.

"If you really love her, you'll let her go," said Arden.

Tim didn't want to hear the truth. "Oh, yeah?" he said, "Just like you let Spirit go?"

The minute the words were out of his mouth Tim could have kicked himself. But it was too late to take them back. With a strangled sob, Arden had already turned away from him and was running toward the house.

Tim turned back to Tawny. The little panther was sitting on the other side of the fence, staring at a bird in her new habitat. She didn't seem interested in Tim anymore.

Tim knew Arden was right — the panther cub really did belong out here, in nature. But why couldn't he be with her, too? As a friend. . . .

His head full of disturbing thoughts, Tim walked slowly back to the house. Thomas Quinn was on the porch waiting.

"Hi, Tim," Gramp called. "Come and watch the sky with me for a minute."

Uh-oh, thought Tim. *Now I'm really going to get yelled at.* He was sure Arden had told on him.

Gramp didn't yell, though. He stood for a long time on the porch, looking at the sun set in the purple sky, before he finally spoke. And then, in the gentlest voice, he said, "You know, Tim, it's a funny thing about being a parent, even a substitute parent. . . .A *good* parent has got to learn to let go. I had to do it with your dad. And your mom and dad are doing it with *you*, too. That's why they sent you here to River Oaks for a whole year.

"And make no mistake, Tim — letting go hurts. It hurts bad. But it's the only way. It's *nature's* way."

Tim stood there, thinking about what Gramp had said. He thought of his par-

97

ents — how they were probably missing him, and Arden and Jesse, just the way he was missing Tawny.

And he knew he missed them, too, just as Tawny was missing him. But then he thought how great it was that Mom and Dad had let him come to River Oaks for the year. . . .

Tim stood there with Gramp, watching the sun disappear and the clouds light up in pink and orange. Neither of them said anything, but Tim was beginning to understand.

Chapter Ten

———•———

Queen of the Wild

The next morning, when it came time for Tim to go feed Tawny, he kept waiting for Gramp or Gran or Arden to say, "I'll come with you."

But nobody said a word. *They still trust me!* Tim thought, relieved.

When he got to the habitat, he spotted Tawny by the fence, right where he'd left her the day before. *She must have stayed there all night*, Tim thought, *wondering where I was*.

He knew he was supposed to go straight down to the blind box and leave her food, but he couldn't help standing there and watching her, just for a moment.

Tawny opened her yellow eyes and found herself staring straight at Tim. Quickly she ran over to where he was standing. It was too late to run away. She'd already seen him.

Well, thought Tim, the damage was already done. What harm could there be in petting her, just once more, now that she already knew he was there? Tim reached out, and Tawny put her paws up on the fence so she could rub her face against his hand.

But suddenly she jumped down from the fence and took off, her sharp claws accidentally scratching Tim's arm.

"Ouch!" he cried.

As he stood there, nursing his wound, Tawny bounded over to a clump of high grass and began circling round it.

At first Tim didn't realize what was happening. Then he saw the snake. It came slithering out from under the grass, heading for a crack in a big rock. But Tawny got there first, pinning the snake under her paw.

She's hunting! Tim realized. Tawny's first lunge pinned the snake for less than a second. The young cub was still only a beginner. It took three lunges before the snake stopped wriggling. Then Tawny proudly hoisted it in her mouth and took her kill off to the rock to eat.

"She's got it!" Tim shouted out loud, running back toward the house. "Gran! Gramp! Hey, everybody!"

He ran into his grandfather about halfway to the house. "Whoa, there, young fella," Gramp said. "What's going on?"

"It's Tawny, Gramp. She killed a snake!"

Thomas Quinn nodded and smiled. "Tim, I'm mighty proud of you," he said. "Tawny's going to make it, thanks to you. Someday, she'll be a truly wild creature, living the life nature meant her to live. And all because you were able to give her up. You're a real 'animals man' now, Tim. You did what was best for the animal, not for yourself."

Tim was silent. He knew he'd almost

blown it. If that snake hadn't come along when it did, he would have been petting Tawny right now, ruining everything.

But he also knew that it was over now. He would never hold the little panther, or cuddle her, or even call her again. For *Tawny's* sake.

Tim and Gramp walked back to the house together. Tim felt very serious, and more grown-up than he ever had before.

"Want to go with me on my rounds today?" asked Gramp. "There's a lot of stuff to be learned around here, and a lot of other animals who could use your help."

After a moment's thought, Tim said, "Thanks, Gramp, but could I meet you later? There's something I've got to do first."

"How long will you be?"

"Just a little while."

"Sure," Gramp said. "I'll be down by the aviary. You can meet me there."

As his grandfather headed for the truck,

Tim set off toward the stables. There he found Arden, brushing Glory's coat. When she saw her brother, she turned away.

"Arden," said Tim, "I'm sorry for what I said yesterday. Really sorry. I didn't mean it, honest."

Arden turned to him. "You're really sorry?" she asked.

"Uh-huh. I've learned a lot since yesterday," he said. "And you were right. Everything you said was right."

Arden smiled, and hugged Tim tight. "I guess we've both learned a lot," she said.

"Come on," said Tim, grabbing her hand. "Tawny's started hunting — do you want to see?"

"You bet!" cried Arden.

The two Quinns ran out of the barn together, and down the path to Tawny's enclosure. When they got there, Tawny was busy cleaning her face.

"Well, there *was* a snake," Tim said sheepishly. "I guess it's gone now."

With a sigh of pure contentment,

Tawny fell back on her haunches and stretched in the sun. The muscles under her golden coat rippled as she made herself comfortable on the huge rock and surveyed her territory.

"Oh, Tim, she's so beautiful," murmured Arden. "Look at her."

All at once, Tawny let out a satisfied roar from deep inside her. The small birds kept still as the sound echoed through the trees.

"Listen to her, Arden," Tim said, beaming with pride. "She's the queen of the wild. And she already *knows* it."